C[illegible] Meets Theo

Story by Dawn McMillan
Illustrations by Roberto Fino

Contents

Rigby®
HOUGHTON MIFFLIN HARCOURT
Supplemental Publishers
www.Rigby.com
800-531-5015

Chapter 1

A Bad Fall

At lunchtime Cody said to the new boy,
"You'll like it here, Theo.
We play a lot of sports,
and our teacher, Mr. Collins, is great!
Josh and I are going to kick a ball around.
Do you want to play with us?"

"I'm not very good at playing soccer,"
Theo said.

"We just have fun," said Cody, laughing.
"If you don't want to play, you can watch!"

"Hurry up, you two!" Josh called. "I'll get a ball and meet you outside."

Cody and Theo were halfway down the stairs when, suddenly, Theo slipped and fell.

Theo let out a loud yell
and grabbed his left leg.

"Get a teacher!" Cody shouted
as another boy rushed over
to see what had happened.

Mr. Collins quickly came to help.

"Don't move, Theo," he said quietly as he bent down to check Theo's leg. "I'll call for an ambulance first, and then I'll let your parents know that you have had an accident."

Chapter 2

A Broken Leg

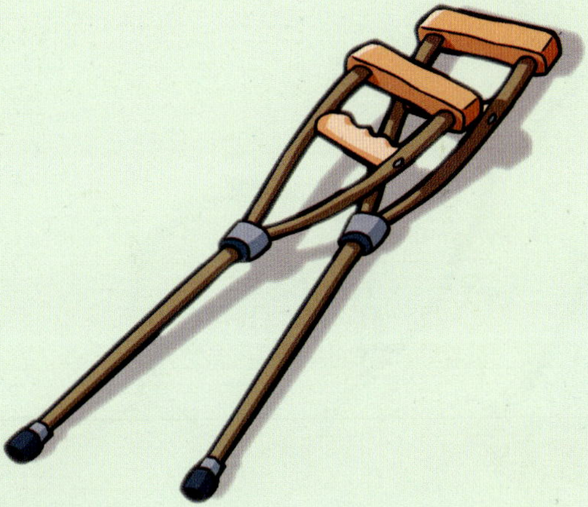

Later that day, Mr. Collins told the class that Theo had broken his leg.
"Theo will be in the hospital for about three days," he said.
"You must all remember to be careful on the stairs."

When Cody got home from school,
he rushed into the kitchen.

"Mom!" he said.
"We have a new boy in our class.
His name is Theo, and he broke his leg
at school today."

"I'm sorry to hear that," said Mom.

"He has to stay in the hospital
for three days," Cody said sadly.
"Can we go and see him, Mom?
I'll take him some of my books."

"Good idea," said Mom.
"But you will have to wait until tomorrow.
Only his family can see him tonight."

Chapter 3

At the Hospital

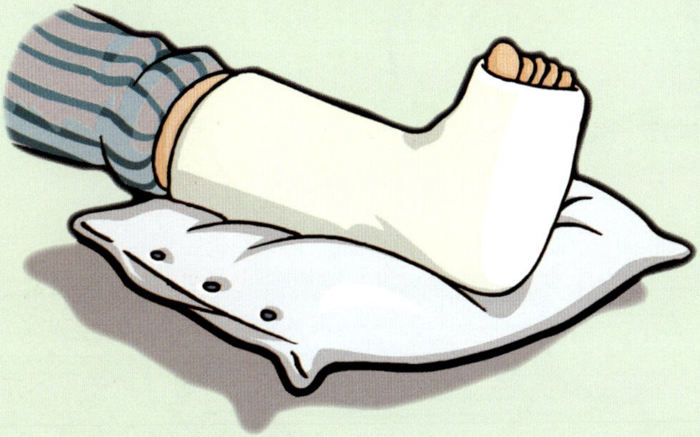

At the hospital the next day,
Cody said, "There he is, Mom."

"He looks tired," said Mom.
"We will just stay for a little while."

"Hi, Theo," said Cody.
"I'm sorry about your leg."

"Hello, Cody," Theo said.
"I've got to have this cast on for weeks!
I can't go swimming
or play soccer with you.
I don't like having a broken leg."

"Don't worry, Theo," Cody said.
"We'll find a lot of things to do together.
I have a big box of games at my house.
When you get out of the hospital,
you can come and play them with me."

Theo looked down and said,
"Hey, Cody! What happened to **your** leg?"

"I was in a car accident when I was four,"
said Cody. "I don't remember much about it."

"Oh," said Theo.

"Your leg will be better in a few weeks, Theo,
but I'll always have to wear this," Cody said.
"It's still a good leg, though!"

"Thanks for the books, Cody,
and for being my friend," Theo said.